A Stormy Night

Written by Andy Blackford
Illustrated by Richard Watson

WAYLAND

It was the middle of the night and Ruby was tucked up in bed.

📞 01628 796969 (library hours)

🌐 www.rbwm.gov.uk/web/onlinelibrary.htm

Please return/renew this item by the last date shown. Books may also be renewed by phone or Internet.

First published in 2010
by Wayland

Text copyright © Andy Blackford
Illustration copyright © Richard Watson

Wayland
338 Euston Road
London NW1 3BH

Wayland Australia
Level 17/207 Kent Street
Sydney, NSW 2000

Series Editor: Louise John
Cover design: Paul Cherrill
Design: D.R.ink
Consultant: Shirley Bickler

A CIP catalogue record for this book is available from the British Library.

ISBN 9780750262163

Printed in China

Wayland is a division of Hachette Children's Books,
an Hachette UK Company

www.hachette.co.uk

Merlin was asleep in his basket.

Suddenly, there was a loud bang! The house shook.

"What was that, Merlin?"
said Ruby.

But Merlin was hiding under
the bed.

Ruby sat up and looked out of the window.

She put on the light.
"Don't worry, Merlin!" she said.
"It's just a storm."

The lightning flashed and the
thunder rumbled.

The rain came down and
Merlin began to howl.

Lulu the cat came running in...

...and so did Bobby the rabbit!

The animals jumped up onto
the bed.

Just then, the lights went out.

"Oh, no!" said Ruby.
"Someone is missing!"

She ran out of the room.

Ruby jumped back into bed
and Dad came in with his torch.

"Are you OK, Ruby?" he said.
"Don't worry. It's just a storm."

"I'm OK, Dad," said Ruby,
"but all the animals
were scared!"

"Ruby," said Dad, "what's that funny bump in your bed?"

Dad pulled back the bed
covers and began to laugh.

"Flipper was scared, too!"
said Ruby.

The storm was soon over.

"Go to sleep, Ruby," said Dad.
"Come on, everyone, let's go
back to bed!"

START READING is a series of highly enjoyable books for beginner readers. **The books have been carefully graded to match the Book Bands widely used in schools.** This enables readers to be sure they choose books that match their own reading ability.

Look out for the Band colour on the book in our Start Reading logo.

The Bands are:

Pink Band 1A & 1B

Red Band 2

Yellow Band 3

Blue Band 4

Green Band 5

Orange Band 6

Turquoise Band 7

Purple Band 8

Gold Band 9

START READING books can be read independently or shared with an adult. They promote the enjoyment of reading through satisfying stories supported by fun illustrations.

Andy Blackford used to play guitar in a rock band. Besides books, he writes about running and scuba diving. He has run across the Sahara Desert and dived with tiger sharks. He lives in the country with his wife and daughter, a friendly collie dog and a grumpy cat.

Richard Watson was born in 1980 and from as soon as he was able to read and write, he always had his nose in a book and a pen in his hand. After school, Richard went on to study illustration in Lincoln and graduated in 2003. He has worked as an illustrator ever since.